THIS YEAR, TRY A YOUNGER MAN ON FOR SIZE

"Look, Devin, this is cute," I said, standing up and walking back toward the front door. "But you and I both know that this is a bit much. You're way too young for me. Not to mention you're my girlfriend's son."

"I'm your friend's son, that part is true. But who said that I was too young for you? I like you. Hell, you're fly as hell and I wanna get to know you." He walked over to me and stood so close that I backed up and hit my head against the door. He placed his hands above my head. "You really want me to leave? Or do you want me to stay and get snowed in with you?"

Damn, I can't stand that the flesh is weak. "You can stay and we'll talk. But I *will not* be having sex with you."

"Who said anything about sex?" He smiled. "When the time comes for me to hit it, it'll be after you beg me to."

—From "Whatever It Takes" by Tu-Shonda L. Whitaker

KISS THE YEAR
Goodbye

BRENDA L. THOMAS

TU-SHONDA L. WHITAKER

CRYSTAL LACEY WINSLOW

DAAIMAH S. POOLE

POCKET BOOKS

NEW YORK LONDON TORONTO SYDNEY

The sale of this book without its cover is unauthorized. If you purchased this book without a cover, you should be aware that it was reported to the publisher as "unsold and destroyed." Neither the author nor the publisher has received payment for the sale of this "stripped book."

 POCKET BOOKS, a division of Simon & Schuster, Inc.
1230 Avenue of the Americas, New York, NY 10020

This book is a work of fiction. Names, characters, places and incidents are products of the author's imagination or are used fictitiously. Any resemblance to actual events or locales or persons, living or dead, is entirely coincidental.

Whatever It Takes copyright © 2005 by Tu-Shonda L. Whitaker
Every New Year copyright © 2005 by Brenda L. Thomas
Dangerously in Love copyright © 2005 by Crystal Lacey Winslow
My Boo copyright © 2005 by Daaimah S. Poole

All rights reserved, including the right to reproduce this book or portions thereof in any form whatsoever. For information address Pocket Books, 1230 Avenue of the Americas, New York, NY 10020

ISBN-13: 978-1-4165-2709-1
ISBN-10:   1-4165-2709-5

This Pocket Books trade paperback edition December 2006

10 9 8 7 6 5 4 3 2 1

POCKET and colophon are registered trademarks of Simon & Schuster, Inc.

Cover design by Kristin V. Mills
Cover photographs by Timothy Shonnard/Getty Images and
    Bruce Ando/Picture Quest

Manufactured in the United States of America

For information regarding special discounts for bulk purchases, please contact Simon & Schuster Special Sales at 1-800-456-6798 or business@simonandschuster.com

Contents

v